LEFTY'S CHRISTMAS PENNIES

By Wilhelmina Bell

ILLUSTRATED By KRISTYN HANEY

Lefty's Christmas Pennies

Printed in the United States of America

Illustration: Kristyn Haney

Copy Editor: Kathy Tuten

Cover Design: Christina Eudy

Book Design and Typography: Christina Eudy

iCi Printing

4311 - D South Boulevard, Charlotte, NC 28209

To Braelon, Kendrick, and Dylan
My great-grandsons

LEFTY

"Lefty's Christmas Pennies"

Lefty walked with a limp on the sidewalk not too far from his house. His brown corduroy pants with one cuff hanging below his left shoe heel were getting dirty from dragging his left foot on the sidewalk. It was a cool spring day. His brown corduroy cap with a small brim turned to the left side of his head, created a shadow on his face from the sun shining brightly in the sky. On the right side of his face, you could see his jet-black, curly hair sticking out from under his cap. Lefty's dark eyes were his most distinct facial feature, his pupils were as black as coal against the whiteness of his eyes. Mrs. Martin, Lefty's mother, always said, "He inherited his dark eyes from his father."

Mrs. Martin

Lefty was looking for pennies. Every day after school he took walks. He frequently walked alone. It was one way he could get exercise without playing ball with his friends in the park. When his two friends Jerome and Ray walked with him, they would run ahead and call out to him, "Hurry up Lefty, we will be late for the ball game in the park." Lefty knew they would wait for him to catch up, but he felt uncomfortable as they waited for him. They had been friends since kindergarten and now they were all ten years old and in the fifth grade. Occasionally, he tried to walk faster, dragging his left foot without tripping or falling. Lefty knew if he walked too fast he sometimes fell. And he was too embarrassed to show his emotions, in front of Jerome and Ray.

Jerome   Ray

Today, he enjoyed looking for pennies, not only on the sidewalk, but in the grass and hedges on the sides of the apartments and row houses in his neighborhood. He had walked three blocks before he found three shiny new pennies and one very old penny. The date on the old penny was not readable. He put the pennies in his pants pocket, crossed at the corner on the other side of the street before heading back home, hoping to find more pennies before he returned home. It did not happen!

Lefty crossed the street again, after walking an extra block to cross at the light. His mother always told him, "Never cross in the middle of the street, you could get hit by a car." Lefty was surprised when he arrived home, no one was sitting on the steps where he lived with his mother. His father had died from a massive heart attack when he was five years old. His memories of his father were fading from his mind. He remembered he was tall and drove a bus for the city. On his days off from work he sometimes took Lefty for rides on the city buses. Immediately after the death of his father, especially when he saw buses and people getting on and off the bus, he cried. Gradually, the memories faded. And only the photos his mother kept displayed in their first-floor apartment were all the memories he had. He was sure they lived on the first floor because of his limp. His friends Jerome and Ray lived on the second-floor, one flight up from him. He wished he lived on their floor.

Opening the door to his apartment with the key he kept around his neck on a string, he was surprised to hear his mother say, "How many pennies did you find today?" Lefty limped to the kitchen table, took off his cap and said, "Three. Three shiny pennies and one old penny. And guess what!" "What?" said, his mother! "And one lucky penny!" "Why is it lucky?" "It has the date of the year I was born, 1948."

Mrs. Martin said, "Go get your piggy bank and we will put the pennies in your bank." Lefty slid out of his chair and limped towards his bedroom. He picked up a small, glass, amber-colored piggy bank from the top of his dresser and held it close to his chest with both hands. He always felt excited when he had found more than one penny to put in his piggy bank. However, he was so excited, walking too fast he tripped and fell before he reached the kitchen. He started to sob. Mrs. Martin jumped up and held his hand as he stood up, still holding his piggy bank with the other hand. She gave him a hug and a kiss on his cheek. Lefty felt much better.

Lefty always showed his real emotions around his mother, without feeling ashamed if he cried. He had cried often after his father's death, he missed him so much. Once he had sat down at the kitchen table, he placed his piggy bank on the table and dropped his three pennies in one at a time. The 1948 penny he kept out. After all it was his lucky penny. He would place it in his pants pocket every time he looked for more good luck pennies. Mrs. Martin said, "I have four pennies for your bank. From now on for every penny you find I will give you the same number of pennies."

"Look, Mommy, my piggy bank is full," he said one day. She did not tell him she frequently put extra pennies in his bank when he wasn't home. Smiling at her son, she told him "You need a new bank. Tomorrow we will go to the five-and-ten cent store and buy a bigger piggy bank." Lefty was so happy, he had dreams about a new piggy bank when he fell asleep that night.

The next day, his mother took him to the five-and-ten-cents store. Lefty saw a big, pink, ceramic piggy bank sitting on a shelf. The piggy bank's nose was the cutest pink pug nose he had ever seen. The nostrils were large enough for him to see the inside. One red flower was painted on the belly of the bank.

WOW! It was the bank he had to have. His mother paid for the bank, and they rode the city bus back to their apartment. Lefty couldn't wait to get home and place his new piggy bank on his dresser, next to his small, glass, amber-colored piggy bank. However, he could not see the inside of the pink piggy bank. How would he know when the bank was full of pennies?

School was finally out for summer vacation. Lefty and his friends Jerome and Ray loved the summer break. They had so much fun playing marbles together, trading comic books, and going to the park for baseball games. Lefty did not play ball with his friends, but he loved watching them play with other kids in the park. Sometimes as they ran around the bases, he shouted, "Safe" or "Out". His favorite past-time was still looking for pennies wherever he walked.

Lefty was sitting on the steps outside his apartment with Jerome and Ray. They were laughing and joking with each other. Suddenly, they heard a window being raised and Mrs. Caledonia yelled, "Keep the noise down! I can't hear the stories on my radio". Lefty said, "We were only laughing and talking." "You are talking too loud! Go someplace else to talk!"

Lefty looked up at the old lady, who lived alone and evidently did not like children. Lefty asked, "Mrs. Caledonia, do you like cookies?" "Yes! I like cookies." "What kind?" "Chocolate chip." "Do you have any pennies? We will buy you some?" They heard the window slam shut. Laughing, they continued with their shenanigans. Lefty kept thinking about Mrs. Caledonia, and finally said, "Let's go penny hunting." They jumped up, and his two friends started to run down the sidewalk. Lefty shouted, "You can't find pennies running. Walk slowly and look down on the sidewalk, also near the hedges and grass."

They had so much fun when they came home. They counted the pennies they found: twelve pennies between them. His friends asked, "What are we going to do with our pennies?" Jerome announced, "I am going to buy bubble gum or maybe lollipops." Ray likewise said, "I am going to buy Tootsie Rolls." Lefty, who was disappointed in their responses, thought maybe they would save their pennies. "I am going to put my pennies in my new piggy bank." Lefty was quiet. Jerome asked, "Why do you put your pennies in a piggy bank?" "Because, I am saving them to buy my mother's Christmas gift". Ray, said, "It's a long time to save pennies. Besides little boys do not buy Christmas gifts, we get gifts." His friends took off running to the candy store near their houses.

Lefty was feeling rejected. He really wanted to ask his friends to put one of their pennies in his bank; however, he knew he wasn't going to ask them for their pennies. Penny hunting for his mother's Christmas gift was his idea.

He was getting ready to go inside when Mrs. Shannon stopped to chat with him before she entered the building. It was a hot summer day and her curly brown hair was matted to the side of her face. Small beads of sweat were on her forehead. She had taken the bus home and walked the five blocks to their apartment building. Mrs. Shannon and Lefty's mother worked part-time together in the five-and-ten-cent store. Woolworth was its name, but no one in the neighborhood called the store by that name.

Mrs. Shannon

Mrs. Shannon put her small brown bag of groceries on the steps, and sat down to talk to Lefty. She pulled her white dress decorated with small red roses down over her knees and crossed her legs. Wiping the little sweat from her brow, and pushing her hair back from her face, she asked Lefty. "What are you doing sitting here all alone? Where are your friends?" Lefty said, "They went to the candy store." "Why don't you go with them? I can give you some money to buy candy." "No, thank you!"

Mrs. Shannon knew Lefty was very close to his mother. She talked about him a lot. About how he always wanted to help around the house with chores; sweeping the kitchen, drying the dishes that she washed after their meals and taking out the garbage.

Mrs. Shannon said, "I know you save pennies. Your mother told me you put all the pennies you find in your piggy banks. What are you planning to spend your pennies on?" Lefty looked at Mrs. Shannon very intensely with his black-as-coal eyes. The whiteness surrounding his pupils bright as snow. Whiter than she had ever seen them. Lefty smiled, "I am going to buy my mother a diamond necklace for a Christ-mas gift." "Really", she said, "Do you know how much a diamond necklace will cost?" "No! But my mommy said, my daddy was saving his money to buy her one, before he died."

Mrs. Shannon stood up, pulling at her dress, and dusting it off with her hand to remove any dirt or dust. Once she reached her apartment, thoughts of Lefty saving pennies to buy his mother a diamond necklace kept returning to her mind. How can I help Lefty buy his mother's gift? Within seconds, a thought popped into her mind. I've got it! I will hide pennies in different places along the route he walks and some other places where he never looks for pennies. Maybe under rocks near the trees, and the little flower garden at the end of our block. She knew that figuring out a way to tell Lefty how to search for pennies in new places was going to be a challenge.

A few days later she saw Lefty and asked him to walk with her to the store. On the way to the store, she spotted a shiny penny in the flower garden almost hidden close to the rose bush. "Look Lefty. There is a penny!"

Lefty, smiled and thank Mrs. Shannon for seeing the penny in a new place. And she continued to find more pennies under rocks near the trees. Lefty could not believe how many pennies they found. Ten pennies in one day!

Mrs. Shannon had a can full of coins in the back of her closet on the floor. She was saving them for a 'rainy day'. The rainy day was now! Lefty could use her pennies. She had not spent the coins in over a year.

Mrs. Shannon made a plan. She would tell her co-workers about Lefty and she would ask them if they had extra pennies saved in their piggy banks, jars or cans they had been collecting a long time. And she would ask if they'd be willing to spare them for a kid with a heart of gold, mentioning that his father had died when Lefty was young and he wanted to buy his mother a diamond necklace for Christmas. "I know he can't buy a diamond necklace, but he can buy her an imitation diamond necklace."

It wasn't long before Lefty found not only pennies in his expanded search, he also found nickels, and the biggest surprise of all was when he found a dime. He did not share his new penny-hunting places with his friends, but he did tell his mother. Soon his large pink piggy bank was so full that it was too heavy to carry to the kitchen table each time to drop in his change. When he finished dropping in pennies, he pushed it to the back of his dresser near his small, amber glass piggy bank.

Mrs. Martin gave him an empty lard tin can that she washed out to use for his over-expanded penny collection. Lefty loved hearing the pennies hit the bottom the first time he dropped the pennies in the can.

It wasn't long before summer ended and school started again. Walking to school with his friends, they always asked him, "Do you still look for pennies?" "Yes!" Jerome wanted to know how many pennies he had saved? Lefty shrugged his shoulders, "I don't know, haven't counted them."

Jerome and Ray did not know that Lefty had expanded his idea of gift giving. He met a girl in school one day in the lunch room. She was in the fourth grade. He had noticed she frequently wore the same dress and socks to school every day. Lefty thought they were her favorite clothes to wear. She always ate alone. He wondered why and decided he would have lunch with her. He limped over to where she was sitting and sat across from her. "What's your name?" "Lucille." Her voice was so low he could hardly hear her. Lefty noticed her sandwich as she pulled it out of her small brown lunch bag. Only half-of-a-sandwich. No peanut butter and jelly, only butter. Lucille offered him some of her sandwich. "No, thank you. I ate my sandwich already." She took small bites, chewing the bread a long time before swallowing.

Lucille

Lefty still had a half-pint of milk left that he had not opened. "Lucille, do you like milk?" he asked. "Yes." "You can have mine I am full." Lucille opened the milk carton, placed the straw in the carton, took three large sips and the carton was empty. Before Lefty had time to engage in further conversation, the teacher announced lunch time was over and it was time to go back to their different classrooms.

It did not take Lefty long to make friends with Lucille in the lunchroom. Lefty liked everything about Lucille, even though she was different from him in appearance. Her skin was white, in fact pale, compared to his dark-brown skin; her eyes as green as the grass in the summer, his black. His hair was jet-black and her hair reminded him of strawberries. It was long and, in the sun, it was a bright orange color.

Lefty learned Lucille was new to his neighborhood and they lived three blocks apart on opposite sides of the street. Lucille said, "I've seen you in the summer walking up and down the street." She watched him from her window when he walked on her side of the sidewalk. She told Lefty she was not allowed to play outside because she had to help care for her younger brothers. Her brothers included three-year-old twins, and a four-year-old brother. Her father was unable to work.

Lefty learned what he knew about her family when they walked home from school. He no longer walked with Jerome and Ray. They walked on same side of the street where they lived. He did not want his new friend to walk home alone. He told Lucille about his penny hunting, and why he was saving the pennies he found. He admitted it was easier to find pennies when it wasn't winter and cold outside. Sometimes on their walks home, Lucille would find a penny and offer it to Lefty. He refused to accept her pennies. "No Way!" She had too many people in her family. He told her, "Save your pennies to buy yourself some candy." However, Lucille had other plans; she hid her pennies near the rose bushes outside her apartment when he left.

Lefty could not believe his lard tin can was already half full with pennies. He did know his mother frequently dropped pennies in his can when he wasn't home.

It was getting close to Christmas and Mrs. Shannon had promised to take him shopping for his mother's Christmas gift. Also, Mrs. Shannon had shared Lefty's piggy bank story with the priest in her church. The entire congregation began bringing, jars, cans and piggy banks they had in their homes to church for a 'rainy day'. The priest kept all of the glass jars, cans and piggy banks stored in a special locked closet in the church.

Mrs. Shannon knocked on Lefty's apartment door, knowing his mother wasn't home yet from work. Lefty opened the door and Mrs. Shannon said, "We have to talk before your mother comes home. It's only one week until Christmas and I would love to take you shopping, to help you pick out a necklace for your mother." Lefty couldn't contain himself. He said, "Thank you, Mrs. Shannon," as he hugged her around the waist. "How are we going to get the pennies out of the piggy banks without letting her know?" "Leave that to me! I have a plan." Lefty asked, "Are we going shopping in H & S, the big store?" "Of course!"

"I also know Lucille is your new friend so maybe she can come shopping with us," Mrs. Shannon said. Lefty's expression changed to one of sadness. Mrs. Shannon was surprised to see the forlorn expression on his face. Mrs. Shannon said, "What's the matter?" "My friend Lucille can't come shopping with us. She has to stay home and help her mother take care of her little brothers." "Oh! Don't worry I know her family, they attend mass at my church. I'll ask Father Flanagan to intervene. We'll work something out."

Lefty was excited again, because he had a plan for how he was going to spend his piggy bank pennies. The small, glass amber bank probably had enough pennies to buy Mrs. Caledonia's chocolate-chip cookies. The pink piggy bank with the large belly, he was sure, had enough pennies to buy his mother a diamond necklace. And the pennies in the large tin can he was going to give to Lucille. She could use them to buy herself a Christmas gift.

That was his plan! Mrs. Shannon had already talked to his mother and she was pleased that Lefty had someone to take him shopping. She always wondered how she was going to tell him that he did not have enough pennies saved to buy her a real diamond necklace. However, she was also disappointed that he'd asked Mrs. Shannon to help count his saved pennies. Mrs. Martin wanted to see his face light up as they counted his pennies together. But all she truly wanted was for Lefty to be happy. After all, Mrs. Shannon was her and Lefty's friend.

Mrs. Shannon took him shopping in the big H & S Department Store. One thing for sure, he did not have enough pennies to buy a real diamond necklace, but the store sold necklaces made with imitation diamonds that sparkled in the light and were very pretty. Lefty's pink piggy bank had enough pennies, nickels and some dimes to buy the imitation diamond necklace. It even came in a black case lined with red velvet. He thanked Mrs. Shannon for taking him shopping in the big store. He was disappointed Mrs. Shannon could not arrange for Lucille to go Christmas shopping with them. However, she told him she had made plans for Lucille to receive her gift from him on Christmas day. "OK!" he said.

Christmas Eve finally arrived and it was really cold. No snow! Lefty and his friends were disappointed because they wanted snow for Christmas. Playing outside in the cold and throwing snowballs at each other was a favorite pastime during the Christmas holidays. That evening he listened to Christmas music on the radio sitting on the floor near their small Christmas tree with different colored lights shining in the dimly lit room. He placed Mrs. Caledonia's chocolate-chip cookies in the cookie can his mother had given him and placed a red bow on top with a Christmas tag. In his own handwriting, he printed: "Merry Christmas, Mrs. Caledonia. From: Lefty your friend."

Mrs. Shannon told him to bring Lucille's gift to her apartment on Christmas Eve. When he came to church with his mother on Christmas Day, her gift would be at the church. He could give it to her after Mass. His mother placed the lid she had given him on the lard can and Lefty tied a red bow around the can. He placed a Christmas tag on top of the lid that said: "Merry Christmas. To: Lucille, my new friend. From: Lefty, your new friend." The last gift he wrapped was for his mother. Lefty chose silver wrapping paper to wrap his mother's gift that he wrapped when he was alone in his room. The tag said: "To: Mommy, my favorite penny. From: Your favorite penny."

Lefty woke up early Christmas morning. It fell on Wednesday. Christmas always seemed like Sunday to him regardless of the day of week Christmas fell. Lefty and his mother were drinking the hot chocolate his mother had made with small marshmallows on top. It was just right. Not too hot! And not too cold! A sip warmed your throat and the smell of the chocolate filled the living room. It was their favorite drink on Christmas morning as they sat together. The Christmas tree lights were shining brightly in the room. The lights on the tree blinked on and off, and the room had a special glow. Knowing they did not have much time before leaving home for church, his mother said, "It's time to open our gifts." She wanted Lefty to open his gifts first, but he was too excited. His gift to his mother had to be the first one opened.

Lefty was on his knees looking for his mother's gift. He knew exactly where he had placed it near the back of the Christmas tree. He did not want his mother to see her gift from him before Christmas morning. He said to her, "I have a surprise for you." Reaching under the tree and placing the gift behind his back, Lefty told his mother "Close your eyes." Then sitting next to his mother on the couch he said, "Now open your eyes. Merry Christmas!"

Lefty handed her his gift and his mother's eyes swelled with tears when she read the Christmas gift tag. She always knew Lefty had a gift with words, and she could not believe he had used the word penny to describe his feelings for her. Her son was worth all the pennies in the world to her and more. She always considered him to be older than his years.

"Wait! Do not open it yet!" He limped to her bedroom, reached for the hand mirror on her dresser, the one she used when she applied her makeup before leaving for work. Quickly, he returned to the living room. "Now you can open your gift." She was very careful not to tear the silver wrapping paper or ruin the bow.

She planned to add them to her shoebox of keepsakes that she had accumulated since he was born.

Once the wrapping paper was removed she held a black jewelry case in her hands. Where did he get the money to shop in H & S Department Store? Seeing the engraving on the top of the case, his mother's hands were trembling as she opened the case and saw the diamond necklace with individual little diamonds sparkling brightly. Lefty handed his mother the hand mirror. "Mommy, hold the mirror. I will fasten the necklace on your neck." He stood behind his mother as she sat on the couch, placed the necklace around her neck and fastened it. "It's beautiful!" She kissed him and gave him a really big hug. "Now tell me, where did you get the money?"

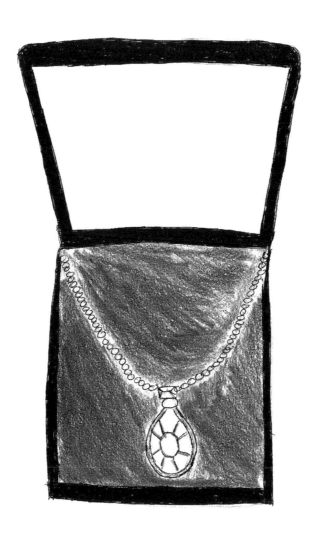

Mommy, Mrs. Shannon took me shopping at the H & S Department Store. She knew my piggy bank had lots of pennies, nickels, dimes and even a couple of quarters, but not enough to buy a genuine diamond necklace. However, the sales lady said that I had enough money to buy an imitation diamond necklace that looked like it was made of real diamonds. "Mommy do you like your imitation diamond necklace?" "Lefty, I will wear it forever. Today I will wear it to mass."

Memories of him when he first called her 'Mommy' flowed through her brain. He was a perfect baby when he was born, except that his left foot turned outward. The doctors said a cast on his left foot would partially correct the problem before he started to walk. However, that wasn't the case. He learned to walk with his limp, was not in pain, and he was just a normal kid with a permanent deformity. The doctor also said, "Several surgeries as he grows may correct his deformity." She remembered the look on his father's face and they made the decision not to have years of surgeries on their son. He did not require crutches and was not in a wheelchair. Lefty was determined to walk on his own, from the first steps he took. They felt God had blessed them with the most beautiful baby boy in the world.

Are you ready to open your gifts from me?" Lefty's mother asked. "Sit on the couch and I will hand them to you one at a time." The first gift was Slinky, a toy he wanted for a long time and had even thought of saving his pennies for one. He could sit outside on the steps of his apartment building and watch it slink down the stairs, from top to bottom without him touching it one time. Slinky was made of springs. He couldn't wait to show it to his friends, especially Lucille.

His second gift was two pairs of pants. Mrs. Martin had a seamstress make the new pants that would not hang below his left shoe and get dirty when he walked. The third gift was in the biggest box under the tree. His mother had purchased a raffle ticket from church and won a small black-and-white TV. Lefty unwrapped the large, heavy box covered with brown paper. He removed the tape from the top and the cardboard sides of the box fell to the floor. "Wow! An RCA TV". He almost tripped as he clapped his hands and jumped up and down and kissed his mother over and over again on the face, forehead and lips.

His friends had televisions but he never asked his mother why they did not have one. He knew her paycheck and his father's Social Security checks were how his mother managed their expenses. Lefty said, "Mommy, this is the best Christmas." After they opened their gifts, they had to hurry and eat breakfast and get ready for church. Christmas Mass at St. Augustine Catholic Church always started on time. Latecomers were seated in folding chairs at the ends of the pews. Lefty and his mother wanted their seats to be together in the pews, not in folding chairs.

Holding hands, they walked the four short blocks to St. Augustine. Lefty wore his new pants and his mother wore her imitation diamond necklace. They entered the church and sat in a pew not too far from the altar. Lefty looked around at the beautiful stained-glass windows and the red carpet extending from the altar to the entrance door. The church was filled with families who lived in his neighborhood. Church bells were ringing, and families were greeting each other with quiet voices, saying "Merry Christmas" and "It's so good to see you Mrs. Martin and Lefty."

His mother did not attend mass every Sunday since her husband had died. She managed to attend special worship services: Easter, Thanksgiving and Christmas. Occasionally she attended weddings, but not often because they reminded her of her own wedding and how happy she had been married to Lefty's father. Never funerals! Tonight, she felt a connection to her former spiritual self. The church felt warm and seeing families together felt good. This was where she really belonged, not just on special worship days, but regularly like she used to.

Lefty's eyes surveyed the religious figures in the small stained-glass windows. After all, St. Augustine church was not familiar to him. Finally, he looked to his left and saw Jerome and Ray standing in the aisle with their families. Ray recognized Lefty and waved to him. Then he saw that Lucille was there with her whole family: mother, father, and three brothers sitting on the same pew. She glanced in his direction and they exchanged waves and smiled at each other.

The bells stopped ringing and the organist played 'O Little Town of Bethlehem'. Lefty knew lots of the words of Christmas songs; they sang them in school in Christmas plays and his mother listened to them on the radio.

Father Flanagan stepped forward to the pulpit and began speaking. Sometimes Lefty could not understand what he was saying. He whispered in his mother's ear, "Is he speaking English?" "Yes and no," she whispered back to him. "He is speaking in Latin and English. Soon he will say everything in English. We have to be quiet." "OK!" Lefty said. The singing was beautiful, but he did not know the prayers and what the crossing of their heart with their hands meant. His mother had not forgotten the rituals of the service and she participated in the Mass, including the words in Latin and making the sign of the cross.

Lefty was kind of glad when the Mass ended. Finally, he could speak to Lucille and meet her family. He was deep in thought when he heard Father Flanagan say, "Please remain seated. We have a special guest with us tonight, Alfred James Martin, Jr." It took a while before he realized Father Flanagan had said his birth name. Only the teachers in school called him Alfred, everyone else called him "Lefty." Father Flanagan said, "Alfred, please stand and come forward." His mother was stunned, she had no idea what was happening and neither did he. He looked to her for directions and she responded; "It's OK, Father Flanagan must have a surprise for you. Lefty slowly stood up and limped to the front of the church. Then, the priest said, "Mrs. Shannon, and Mrs. Martin, please come forward and stand with Alfred."

The priest spoke to the congregation in a soft and caring voice. "Alfred is only eleven years old and he has made a significant difference in one of the families in our church. He looks for pennies while walking to and from school every day and also on weekends. When he finds pennies, he takes them home and puts them in his piggy banks. He started with a very small, glass, amber-colored piggy bank and when it was full his mother took him to the five-and-ten-cent store and brought him a larger pink ceramic bank with a red flower painted on one side. When the pink piggy bank was full, she gave him a large tin lard can to put his pennies in.

Alfred had an angel who spoke to him one day while he was sitting outside on his apartment steps. Who was that Angel? Mrs. Shannon. While she was talking to him, Alfred told her he was saving his pennies to buy his mother a diamond necklace for a Christmas gift. His angel, unbeknownst to him, started hiding her pennies, nickels and occasionally dimes for him to find. She had a good idea. She would give him her can full of coins that she kept in her closet. She was saving them for a rainy day. What's a rainy day? Is it when we have a piggy bank stuffed with pennies that we are not using? Well," Father Flanagan said, "Maybe someone else can use our rainy-day penny collections today."

"Mrs. Shannon had asked the church members if they had rainy-day piggy banks at home to share with someone else. The congregation responded, "Yes!" I will now ask Mrs. Shannon to bring out our church's rainy-day pennies from the back. Alfred will you help Mrs. Shannon?" "Yes." They went through a door and there in the hallway was a table with cans, jars, piggy banks, even a couple of beer bottles with coins filled to the top. Mrs. Shannon and Lefty rolled the table into the church. A Merry Christmas sign hung on the front of the table that had been designed by the children in the church.

Father Flanagan asked the Ryan family (Lucille's family) to stand and come forward. The family stood up and walked to the front of the church: Lucille's mother, father, twins and her other brother. Father Flanagan said, "This is our Christmas gift to your family." Tears fell on Mrs. Ryan's cheeks. Lefty noticed that Lucille had stepped in front of her father, and was using her small hands to speak to him in sign language. Her father was deaf. He was working as a welder when an explosion occurred and he had lost his hearing. Lefty could not believe Lucille never told him her father was deaf. She only said he was not working and her mother needed her to help care for her three-year-old twin brothers.

The congregation stood up and clapped, and started to come forward and hug the family and wish them Merry Christmas. However, Father Flanagan said, "Please remain seated just a little longer. The last gift we have I am going to ask Alfred to present." Lefty was standing with Mrs. Shannon when someone walked in from the hallway carrying his lard can with the big red ribbon tied around it. The person gave the can to Mrs. Shannon and she handed it to Lefty then called Lucille to come forward. Lucille was trembling and crying. Mrs. Shannon whispered to Lefty that he should give her his Christmas gift.

Lefty shifted his body from right to left to keep himself steady. He was so nervous he felt his insides shaking and he was unsure if he could speak at all. He was so embarrassed. Lefty closed his eyes and opened them again and the words came out. "I saved these pennies for my new friend so she can buy herself and her little brothers Christmas gifts." Handing the can to her he said, "Merry Christmas, Lucille". She was speechless for a moment. Her skin turned pale and she felt light-headed. She took Lefty's hand in hers and said, "Thank you, Lefty." Once again members and friends came forward and hugged Lucille and Lefty. When he looked over at his mother she was making the sign of the cross. The priest instructed Lucille, Mrs. Shannon and Lefty to sit on the front pew.

The priest said, "From this Christmas on, St. Augustine will be 'The Piggy Bank Give-away Church,' not just for our own members, but for anyone in the neighborhood." Father Flanagan gave the benediction and with that, Christmas Mass at St. Augustine Church was over. The organist played 'Jingle Bells' as the congregation exited the church. Lefty waved goodbye to Lucille and her family and Mrs. Shannon walked home with Lefty and his mother.

When they arrived at their apartment Lefty's mother asked him, "Did you enjoy Mass?" "Yes, Mommy, a whole lot!" "I think we'll start going to Mass every Sunday." "Do I have to learn Latin?" Lefty asked. Smiling at him, his mother said, "Of course not, at least not until you are confirmed."

Once they were in their apartment Lefty admitted, "Mommy, I almost forgot that I have to give Mrs. Caledonia her Christmas gift." "You can take it to her now." Lefty picked up the cookies and walked across the hall and knocked on her door. "Who is it?" "Lefty!" "Go away little boy. It's Christmas so please do not bother me." "I have something for you. Should I leave the chocolate-chip cookies outside your door?" He held his ear close to the door and heard movement. Finally, the door opened and there was Mrs. Caledonia still in her nightgown and robe. "Can I come in?" "I guess so."

Lefty held out the cookie can and asked, "What are you doing?" "Listening to my radio." Lefty said, surprised, "In the dark!" Mrs. Caledonia responded, "Who needs light?" "I do, so I can give you these chocolate-chip cookies for Christmas." Mrs. Caledonia turned on the lamp near her chair and raised the window shade. "Is this enough light for you? "Yes!" he said and gave her the can of cookies. "Merry Christmas." She took the cookies and smiling pulled the lid off the can. "Your mother baked these cookies?" "No! I saved my pennies to buy you those chocolate chip cookies." Smiling again she said, "You are a sweet little boy," and asked, "Do you want one, Lefty?"

He was surprised that she called him by his name. Lefty knew, then, she actually liked him. He had gained another new friend. "Yes, I will have one cookie if you eat one with me." Mrs. Caledonia said, "Let's sit at the kitchen table and have our cookies with some cold milk." "Mrs. Caledonia, maybe sometimes I will come and sit with you while you listen to your radio." Then, rising he said, "I have got to go now. Merry Christmas again Mrs. Caledonia. Don't forget to read my Christmas tag."

On the way back to his apartment Lefty shouted, "Merry Christmas, everyone." He couldn't wait to tell his Mommy all about his Christmas visit with Mrs. Caledonia.

About the illustrator...

Kristyn Haney, my seventeen-year-old great-grand-niece lives in Valley Stream, NY and attends Long Island Lutheran Middle and High School, Brookville, NY. My early memory of her as an elementary school student is that she always came home with beautiful drawings that she had made. Animals, flowers, her environment and people were her subjects. Kristyn's interest in art continues and is still one of her favorite activities. She is an Honor Roll student and her plans are to attend college after high-school graduation.

Wilhelmina Bell was born in Brooklyn, New York. She received a B.S. degree from the State University of New York, New Paltz, NY and she is retired from the New York State Office of Mental Retardation and Disabilities.

This is my debut children's book. The idea for writing "Lefty's Christmas Pennies" came from my own practice of being kind to others. The COVID-19 pandemic was the first time in my life that I was unable to donate Christmas gifts to agencies that collected them for children. This past Christmas when the coins I saved in my little wooden bank at home was full, I rolled the coins and took them to the bank. The amount was $74.00. I gave it all to a family I did not know that lives in a public housing development near my home. The mother could not believe a total stranger rang her doorbell and handed her a Christmas card with $74.00 in cash! She asked me my name and I said, "My name is not important. Merry Christmas to you and your children." Then I drove away.

Kindness and compassion should always be extended and my story of "Lefty Christmas Pennies" is a tangible example.

I am a mother, grandmother and great-grandmother. I live in Charlotte, NC with my husband.

Contact Wilhelmina Bell for readings and signings.
email: minaoct@aol.com

Contact Wilhelmina Bell for readings and signings.

Email: minaoct@aol.com

Made in the USA
Columbia, SC
20 September 2022

67417260R00020